MEET THE SACCONEJOLYs

Hi Friends!

Jonathan

Anna

Emilia

Eduardo

Alessia

AND THEIR FRIENDLIEST FRIENDS

Sina

Albi

Bianca

Nuvies

To Albi, Sina, Nivea, Theo, Nuvies and Bianca for being
the best doggy friends and inspiring me to write this book.
To Anna's family cats Smudge, Oreo and Miffy, thanks for being the best cat-naps!
To my human kids, Emilia, Eduardo and Alessia, you inspire me every day.
To my wife and best friend, Anna, without you being a super mom this book
would never have been written. And finally to you, the person reading this,
thank you for supporting me. – J.S.J.

To Leonardo – F.G.

EGMONT

We bring stories to life

First published in Great Britain 2017 by Egmont UK Limited,
The Yellow Building, 1 Nicholas Road, London W11 4AN

www.egmont.co.uk

Copyright © Little Squid Media ULC, 2017

Illustrated by Francesca Gambatesa
Photographs taken by Greg Hammond

The moral rights have been asserted.

ISBN 978 1 4052 8865 1

NO CATS,
DOGS OR
SQUIRRELS
WERE HARMED
IN THE
MAKING OF
THIS STORY.

THE SACCONEJOLYS
AND THE GREAT CAT-NAP

Written by Jonathan Saccone Joly

Illustrated by Francesca Gambatesa

EGMONT

There were three children called
Emilia, Eduardo and Alessia.
They had six white furry dogs
and they did **everything** together . . .

...dressing up
as **pirates**,

dressing up
as **princesses**

and dressing up as **ballerinas**.
(They really were FANTASTIC
at dressing up!)

And they loved
dancing...

. . . especially when Emilia and Eduardo
came home from school!

One night, Emilia asked Dad to read her a new story
she'd borrowed from the library.

It was called . . .

I'd Really Like to Have a Cat

After the story, Dad gave Emilia her night-night kiss.
As she drifted off to sleep, she whispered . . .

"I'd really like
to have a cat."

And fell fast asleep!

Bianca was so shocked
that she ran off to tell
the others,

"Emergency meeting, lads!"

"Why on earth does she want
a cat?!" said Nuvies.
"Everyone knows that
dogs are the best pets!"

"Oh dear!"
said Sina. "What can
we do to help Emilia?"

"It's easy peasy," said Bianca.
"You know those three cats
who live nearby?"

"Smudge, Miffy
and Socks?" said
Albi, nervously.

"That's them," said Bianca.
"Well, it's time for
THE GREAT CAT-NAP!"

In no time at all, Bianca had the whole thing planned out.

THE GREAT CAT-NAP

Step One:
find a cat

Step Two:
play amazing
trick on cat

Step Three:
CAT-NAP
CAT!

And she split the dogs into three teams:

TARGET: SMUDGE
TEAM 1:
THEO AND SINA
CHANCE OF SUCCESS:
NONE AT ALL

TARGET: MIFFY
TEAM 2:
ALBI AND NIVEA
CHANCE OF SUCCESS:
HMMM, MAYBE

TARGET: SOCKS
TEAM 3:
BIANCA AND NUVIES
CHANCE OF SUCCESS:
100% EASY PEASY

The next morning, they waited until the children had gone to school, then . . .

Team One went first.

"Everyone likes food," said Theo.
So he and Sina sprinkled some scrummy biscuits
next to Smudge's cat flap. And waited.

Smudge came out of the
cat flap and took a bite.
But . . . BLEURGH!
He didn't like dog treats,
and spat them out again!

Sina woofed,
"He's going back in again!
Don't let him get away!"

Theo raced for the cat.

But he tripped over the
rest of the dog biscuits
and went head first
into the cat flap.
BOING!

FAIL

So it was Team Two's turn to cat-nap.

Albi and Nivea put one of Emilia's
cuddly toys near where Miffy
was sunbathing and hid.

"Oh, Miffy!" said Nivea, trying to do a stripy voice.
"It's Tara, your cousin from India!
I've come for a *purrfect* visit.
Please come over and say hello."

Miffy took one look at the tiger . . .

. . . and yowled, "Waaaaaaaah!"

Miffy looked so upset that Albi asked her what was wrong.

"I'm terrified of tigers," Miffy sobbed.

"You poor thing!" said Albi.

The dogs felt so sorry for Miffy that they dried her eyes, gave her cuddles and took her back to her house.

And totally forgot they were supposed to be cat-napping her! Oops!

FAIL

Team Three were bound to succeed. Bianca and Nuvies
spent forever working out a plan to cat-nap Socks.

Their plan was so brilliant, Socks would never get away!
They got two nets and waited round a corner to catch the cat . . .

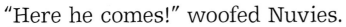

"Here he comes!" woofed Nuvies.
"Let's get him!"

But Socks heard her and ran round the corner so fast that he was out of the way when Bianca and Nuvies swooped with their nets . . .

Oops!
They caught one another instead.

"Get your net off me!" growled Bianca.

"You get your net off me first!" fumed Nuvies.

The Great Cat-Nap had failed.

"What are we going to do?" said Bianca.

"Emilia wants to have a cat and we've messed up big time!"

"We are the worst friends ever!" said Albi.

"You're the silliest friends more like!" a small squirrel chuckled.
He'd been enjoying the entertainment all day.
"There's a very easy way for you to give Emilia
all the cats she could ever want."

"But we're rubbish at cat-napping!" said Albi, sadly.

The squirrel rolled his eyes.
"What's the thing you are all fantastic at?"

"Eating!" said Theo,
through a mouthful
of dog biscuit.

"Dancing!"
said Nuvies.

"Dressing up!" said Bianca.
"Of course! Come on, everyone, I've got an idea.
There's not much time!"

It was called . . .

saccone JOLYs

THE STORY BEHIND THE STORY!

Inspiration behind the story

I wonder if the dogs will like the book?

Emilia gasped – it was the dogs all along!
"You are the best pets EVER!" she said.

Testing out our bedtime story

Story development

Working with my editor

The big reveal!